The Lighthouse Keeper's Stories

Ronda & David Armitage

SCHOLASTIC

The Lighthouse Keeper's Lunch first published in
the UK in 1977 by Andre Deutsch Ltd.
The Lighthouse Keeper's Picnic first published
in 1993 by Scholastic Publications Ltd.
This edition first published in 2008 by Scholastic Children's Books
Euston House, 24 Eversholt Street
London NW1 1DB
a division of Scholastic Ltd
www.scholastic.co.uk
London ~ New York ~ Toronto ~ Sydney ~ Auckland
Mexico City ~ New Delhi ~ Hong Kong

JS

The Lighthouse Keeper's Lunch

Once there was a lighthouse keeper called Mr Grinling. At night time he lived in a small white cottage perched high on the cliffs.

In the day time he rowed out
to his lighthouse on the rocks
to clean and polish the light.

Mr Grinling was a most
industrious lighthouse keeper.
Come rain…

…or shine, he tended his light.

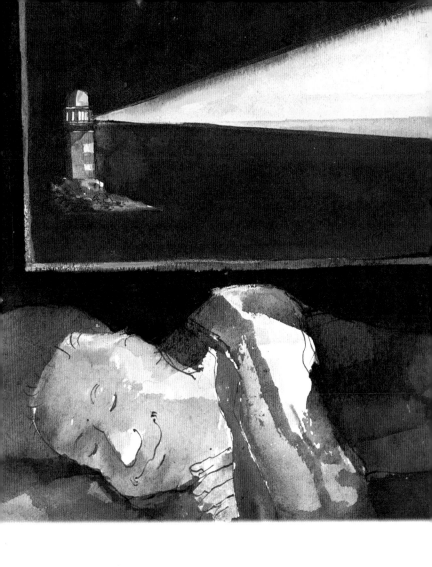

Sometimes at night, as Mr
Grinling lay sleeping in his
warm bed…

…the ships would toot to tell him that his light was shining brightly and clearly out to sea.

Each morning while Mr Grinling polished the light, Mrs Grinling worked in the kitchen of the little white cottage on the cliffs concocting a delicious lunch for him.

Once she had prepared the lunch she packed it into a special basket and clipped it onto a wire that ran from the little white cottage to the lighthouse on the rocks.

But one Monday something terrible happened. Mrs Grinling had prepared a particularly appetising lunch.

She had made…

A Mixed Seafood Salad

A Lighthouse Sandwich

Cold Chicken Garni

2 Sausages and Crisps

Peach Surprise

Iced Sea Biscuits

Drinks and Assorted Fruit

She put the lunch in the basket as usual and sent it down the wire.

But the lunch did not
arrive. It was spotted by three
scavenging seagulls who set
upon it and devoured it
with great gusto.

   "Clear off, you varmints,"
shouted Mr Grinling, but
the seagulls took not the
slightest notice.

That evening Mr and Mrs Grinling decided on a plan to baffle the seagulls.

"Tomorrow I shall tie the napkin to the basket," said Mrs Grinling.

"Of course, my dear," agreed Mr Grinling. "A sound plan."

On Tuesday evening Mr and Mrs Grinling racked their brains for another plan.

"They are a brazen lot, those seagulls," said Mrs Grinling.

"Brazen indeed," said Mr Grinling. "What shall we do?"

"Our cat does not appear to like seagulls," said Mrs Grinling.

"No, my dear," said Mr Grinling. "Hamish is an accomplished seagull chaser."

"Of course!" exclaimed Mrs Grinling. "Tomorrow Hamish can guard the lunch."

"A most ingenious plan," agreed Mr. Grinling.

Hamish did not think that this plan was ingenious at all. He spat and hissed as Mrs Grinling secured him in the basket.

"There, there, Hamish," said Mrs Grinling consolingly, "I'll have a tasty piece of herring waiting for you when you arrive home."

Sadly, flying did not agree with Hamish. His fur stood on end when the basket swayed, his whiskers drooped when he peered down at the wet, blue sea and he felt much too sick even to notice the seagulls, let alone scare them away from the lunch.

"Lackaday, lackaday," said Mr Grinling sadly.

"Miaow, miaow," agreed Hamish pitifully.

On Wednesday evening Mr and Mrs Grinling racked their brains again for a new plan.

"What shall we do?" said Mr Grinling. Mrs Grinling looked thoughtful.

"I have it!" she exclaimed. "Just the mixture for hungry seagulls."

"Indeed, my dear," said Mr Grinling. "What have you in mind?"

"Wait and see," said Mrs Grinling, "just wait and see."

"Mustard sandwiches," chuckled Mr Grinling. "A truly superb plan, my dear, truly superb."

On Thursday morning
Mrs Grinling carefully packed
the mustard sandwiches and
sent them off down the wire
to the expectant seagulls.

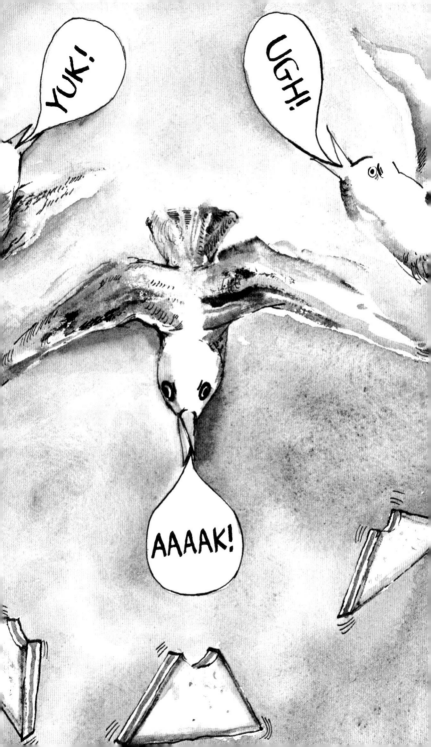

On Friday Mrs Grinling
repeated the mustard mixture.

So, on Saturday, up in the little white cottage on the cliffs, a jubilant Mrs Grinling put away the mustard pot before she prepared a scrumptious lunch for Mr Grinling.

While he waited for his lunch down in the lighthouse on the rocks, Mr Grinling sang snatches of old sea shanties as he surveyed the coastline through his telescope…

… and this is what he saw…

"Ah well, such is life," mused Mr Grinling as he sat down to enjoy a leisurely lunch in the warm sunshine.

The
Lighthouse
Keeper's Picnic

Mr Grinling was a lighthouse
keeper. He lived with his wife, Mrs
Grinling, and their cat, Hamish, in
a little white cottage on the cliffs.

When he was a younger man
Mr Grinling used to row out to

the lighthouse every morning to clean and polish the light.

Now he had an assistant called Sam. Some days Mr Grinling was the lighthouse keeper and some days it was Sam.

On his days off there were lots of things Mr Grinling liked to do.

He liked playing hide and seek with Hamish, he liked growing geraniums and heliotropes,

he liked singing loudly in the village choir but, most of all, he liked eating.

Breakfast, lunch and dinner and a few little snacks in between. Eating was what he did best. Sometimes while he ate he would hum a little tune.

Mrs Grinling worried about the eating.

"Mr G, don't you think perhaps you're just a bit too rotund?" she asked. "I don't know how you're going to run races at the village picnic tomorrow." Mr Grinling gazed at himself in the mirror.

"Nonsense, Mrs G," he said as he did up his shirt. But he went outside to practise his running before dinner.

Mr Grinling loved the village picnic. All the villagers came. Big ones and little ones, running and skipping, huffing and puffing. Mrs Grinling always prepared a splendid picnic spread and she always kept it as a surprise.

The picnic day started badly for the Grinlings. They woke up at 9 o'clock instead of 8 o'clock. In the rush Mr Grinling tripped over Hamish. Hamish hid behind the sofa.

They were half way across the bay before they remembered he was still at home and halfway across again when they remembered the second lunch basket.

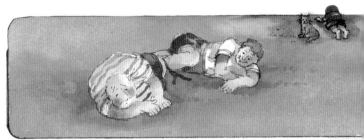

They were very late for the picnic and they forgot to tie up the dinghy.

Everybody was lining up for the egg and spoon race when they arrived.

Mr Grinling ran as fast as he was able but he still came last. He and Joe Jenkins tripped over each other in the three-legged race. As for the last race he couldn't even fit in the sack, let alone jump.

Mr Grinling was very upset. He stomped off to swim by himself before lunch. He lay on his back with his tummy in the air. Up above a rainbow balloon drifted.

Mr Grinling sighed. That would be the life, floating just like a cloud, that's what he'd really like to do. He sang a floating song to himself.

High in the sky
Gently cruising,
Wrapped up in cotton wool
Quietly musing,
Singing a cloud song.

The picnic lunches were magnificent. Mr Grinling wandered about tasting – a little bit here, a little bit there.

But he stopped quite still when he saw Mrs Grinling's spread.

Naughty Nibbles

Bumper Bites

Tempting Treats for Tinies

Melon Boat
Limpet Log
Lighthouse Cake
Salad Crab
Great Green Whale Jelly
Cream Whorls
Starfish Sandwiches
Scallop Sausages
Sea Food

"Sea food" she had called it and it was beautiful. Mr Grinling ate a piece of everything.

"Delicious and delectable," he announced with his mouth full of green whale jelly.

"The best cook here today, Mrs G, possbly the best cook in the whole, wide world."

Once the picnic was eaten everyone was too full to run or jump any more. Most of the villagers packed up their baskets, and went happily home. Mr and Mrs Grinling felt like a rest.

Hey! Buzz off, Bert- this is mine!

They lay in the sun with their heads under their hats and quietly snored.

When they awoke the sun was beginning to fade, the tide was coming in and the dinghy had floated away.

Don't you 'fat cat' me!

Gosh! Old fat cat can move!

Drat that cat! He's spoilt our lunch.

"Well, that's that," said Mrs Grinling, "we'll just have to walk home." Mr Grinling groaned.

They set off around the rocks. In and out, up and down they went, over and under, rock after rock. Soon the sun had disappeared. The water came closer.

"We must hurry, Mr G," said Mrs Grinling. "The tide is racing in."

But Mr Grinling couldn't hurry.

"I can't climb any more," he puffed, "and I certainly can't climb through that hole, I'll get stuck." Mrs Grinling looked at the hole and she looked at Mr Grinling's tummy.

"In that case there's nothing for it," she said. "We'll have to stay here till morning."

They found a flat rock and huddled together to keep warm. The moon came up. The water rose. Once a wave splashed their feet a little but it was only one and then the water began to go down.

Sam was surprised to see the lighthouse light still shining next morning. When he saw the dinghy nudging against the jetty below he guessed what had happened. He gazed round the bay. Yes, there they were; jumping up and down and waving.

He set off right away to rescue them.

Mrs Grinling was cross. Mr Grinling didn't think he'd ever seen her quite so cross.

"Mr Grinling," she glared, "that was the coldest and most frightening night I have ever had, and all because you're so fat!"

Mr Grinling sighed, "You're quite right, Mrs G, I am too fat. What shall I do?"

"Well," said Mrs Grinling, "the cakes will have to go AND the chocolates, the crisps and the sweets."

Mr Grinling was horrified: all his favourite foods.

He worked very hard at getting
thinner. He ran up and down the
path from the little white cottage
to the dinghy.

He cycled like the wind into the village and home again.

Some nights he was so tired that he fell asleep in his dinner.

But he did miss the little snacks.

"Just one chocolate biscuit, Mrs G?" he pleaded.

"No, Mr G," she said firmly, "Not even half of one."

Sam didn't like it when Mr Grinling was unhappy.

"I'll get you a little something," he whispered. "Mrs Grinling need never know."

Mr Grinling hid the snacks very carefully, and he ate only one thing each day.

But when Mrs Grinling told him to climb on the scales, he was as heavy as ever.

"I don't understand," said Mrs Grinling. "You've been so good, no chocolates or biscuits." Mr Grinling gazed at the ceiling.

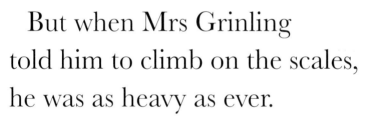

For the next few days Mrs Grinling watched Mr Grinling very closely. She spied from behind the door when he crept into the living room.

"Got you, Mr Grinling!' She pounced as his hand reached into the vase. "You should be ashamed of yourself." Mr Grinling hung his head.

"Promise me," said Mrs Grinling, "no more snacks."

Mr Grinling sighed, "I promise, Mrs G."

Mr Grinling went on trying to get thinner. One day when he was out cycling with Hamish he saw the rainbow balloon again. It was so close he could hear the gentle roar.

"I'd love to float like that," he thought, "as light as a feather. But then I'm not light." He looked at his round tummy. "I don't suppose I'd even fit in the basket," he said gloomily.

He told Mrs Grinling about the balloon that evening.

"Not for you, Mr G," she said, "they'd never get you off the ground."

Mr Grinling got a surprise in
the village next day. He saw
a large notice in a house window.
He knocked at the door.

"I don't suppose I'd be able
to have a ride in your balloon?"
he asked.

BALLOON
RIDES

The balloon lady gazed at him, then slowly she walked round him both ways.

"Of course you can," she said, "and we could probably take Mrs Grinling as well." Mr Grinling smiled, a great beaming smile.

So that's how the Grinlings went floating one fine afternoon. Hamish and Sam waved them goodbye.

Up and over the lighthouse they went and across the bay. Past the rock where they'd spent that cold night, over the sea where the whales dived and played, over the cliffs where the seagulls nested.

And then the land was below, houses and barns; cows, sheep and horses.

Mr Grinling smiled at
Mrs Grinling.
   "This is the best thing
I have ever done," he said.
"It's even better than eating."

High in the sky
Gently cruising,
Wrapped up in cotton wool
Quietly musing,
Singing a cloud song.